Ralf.

Jean Jullien

Original idea and illustrations by
Jean Jullien

Text collaboration by
Gwendal Le Bec

Frances Lincoln
Children's Books

LANCASHIRE COUNTY LIBRARY

D0317923

30118134055415

Ralf is a little dog...

... who takes up a lot of space!

He creeps into bed and barks,

"Goodnight!"

... but hardly ever in the right spot.

"Stop getting under our feet!"
we are always shouting.

But Ralf doesn't
mean to cause
trouble.

It's just that his long body gets in the way all the time.

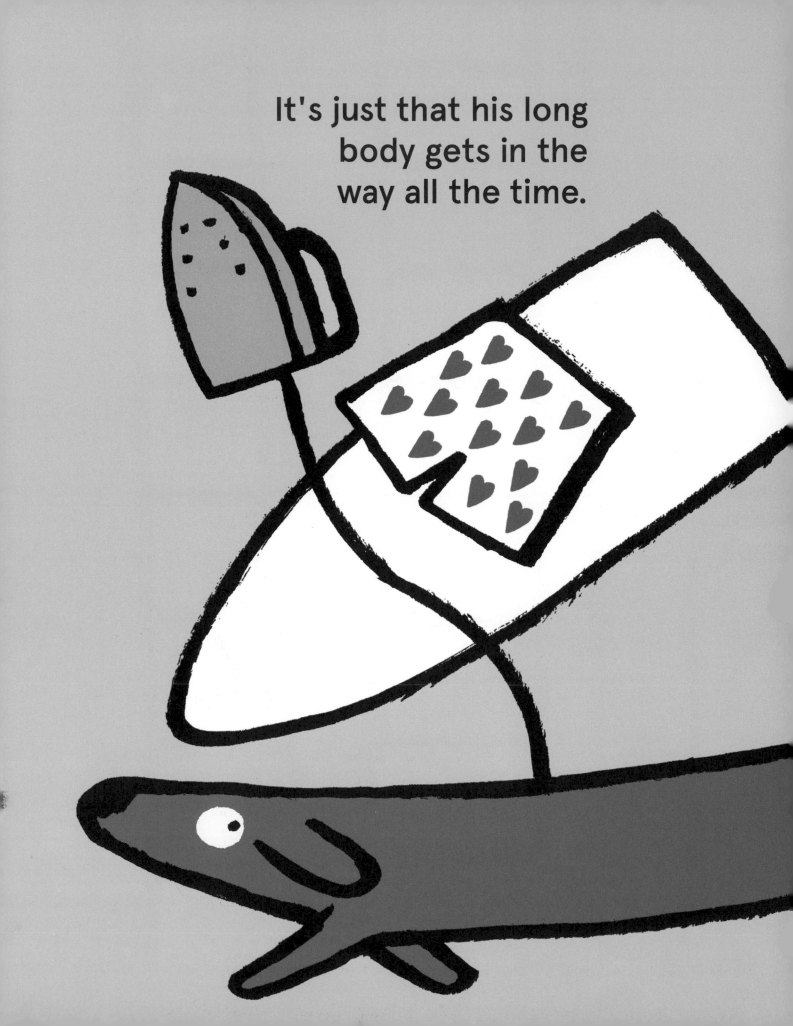

It drives Dad mad.

When he is in his kennel,
everything is quiet.

Maybe a bit too quiet...

Sniff! Sniff!
The smell of smoke
tickles his nose.

Quickly! Ralf runs into the house to see what's going on.

"Ouch!"
His bottom gets stuck
in the door.

But if he doesn't
do something,
the house will
burn down!

Ralf pulls so hard that his body begins to stretch.

Everyone is
fast asleep!
What can he do?

Ralf runs to get help.
His body stretches
like rubber.

"Our house is on fire!"
he barks at the fireman.

NEE-NAW! NEE-NAW!
The firefighters race
through the night.

"Help! Help!"

WHOOSH!
Ten seconds
later, everyone
has escaped the
burning house.

Now, Ralf
is a very very
long dog...